W9-BKZ-232

JOLLY OLD SANTA CLAUS

Illustrated by
GEORGE HINKE

Told in Verse by
ALICE LEEDY MASON

*To My Four
Grandchildren*

CHILDRENS PRESS, CHICAGO
School & Library Edition

"Ho, Ho," laughed Jolly Old Santa Claus
As he stroked his beard all white.
"Come, brownies! Come, Mrs. Santa,
I've something to read you tonight."

Mrs. Santa stopped playing the carols
The brownies had asked her to play,
For she saw Santa Claus had a letter
That had just arrived by sleigh.

"What does it say? Where is it from?
Did it come from a boy or a girl?"
"Whoa there," Old Santa answered—
"Our mail comes from the whole wide world!

"This letter is from a good little boy
Who helps around the house.
He's nice to his brothers and sisters
And takes care of his own pet mouse.

"The question he wants us to answer
Is not about presents I'll bring.
He asks if we at the North Pole
Are busy with anything!"

"Are we!" shout the brownies.
Their voices ring like song.
"We're terribly busy at Christmas—
And we work hard all year long."

(If you're quiet, we'll visit their workshop.
When you see it, you'll hardly believe
How busy the brownies are. Will they
Be ready by Christmas Eve?)

"It's O.K.," says Santa Claus gaily.
"Just don't let the brownies see!
We'll watch them making cookies —
They're as busy as busy can be.

"They are mixing big bowls of batter
Made of milk and eggs and flour.
Rolling and shaping and cutting
Hundreds of cookies an hour."

Old Grandpa Brownie just fell down;
His glasses are lost, too!
I think he's trying to do too much —
But there's so much left to do!

See Jingles on top of the oven.
He makes sure the cookies don't burn.
They're like stars, and hearts, and
    gingerbread boys —
Each tray must have
    its own turn.

Brownies like to make
    Christmas cookies.
Some are humming a
    Christmas song.
But let's not stay in the kitchen —
We'd best be hurrying along.

The next shop we're scheduled to visit
Is the toy shop — a wonderful place!
All are busy except Lazy Brownie.
What a silly look on his face!

He's taking a ride on the rock-a-bye horse
When he should be helping his friend.
He isn't lazy all of the time;
Santa knows he will help in the end.

Right now Santa is checking his toy list.
It grows longer and longer each day.
Airplanes and drums; teddy bears, dolls…
And others not yet on display.

There's Lady Whiskers, Santa's favorite cat.
Grandpa Brownie has tripped on the stairs.
Other brownies are painting and
                    working quite hard
                Making their bright-
                colored wares.

Soon the clock will strike midnight!
Take a look at the clock on the wall.
Chief Brownie knows what to do —
He's giving the "hurry-up" call.

While brownies clean up the toy shop,
And before they give us a broom,
Let's hurry down for a close-up look
At Santa's own
   "Christmas Tree Room."

24
December

GOOD BOYS AND G

Oh! What a lovely sight!
Our ornaments are made right here.
See the brownies back in the corner
Blowing bubbles of glass bright
  and clear.

Impy Brownie by that box of sand
Is painting and dipping each one.
He's eager to make each one perfect.
I think that his job would be fun.

Lazy Brownie still isn't working!
He's sitting high up on a shelf.
Soon Jolly Old Santa will call him,
Saying, "Lend me a hand, little elf."

Christmas time is approaching.
Piles of ornaments and gifts
  are growing.
Is Santa about to leave?
Let's find out where he's going.

Why this must be Santa's Office!
The letters are scattered about.
Santa reads what the children are saying.
Are they good or bad? He will find out.

Helper Brownie is marking the chart under "bad."
I hope that mark isn't for you.
Mrs. Santa is checking addresses;
Of new ones she has
more than a few.

On Santa's chair sits Lady Whiskers.
Lazy Brownie is safe out of sight —
He's blowing smoke rings and not working —
Now, do you think this is right?

Jingles and Impy Brownie
Open letters for Santa to read.
Chief Brownie is tugging a mail sack,
Wondering what else Santa may need.

Look at Santa. He's reading a letter
That came from a good girl or boy.
Is it your letter he's reading?
Did you ask for
your favorite toy?

Now the trees seem to be ready.
They're snowy and fresh and green.
Soon they'll be in people's houses —
The most beautiful trees to be seen.

While sawing, the brownies sing carols.
Forest animals slowly draw near.
They like to watch brownies at work;
Brownie singing is lovely to hear.

Old Grandpa Brownie has fallen.
His glasses are lost in the snow!
He was rushing to load up the trees
And fell in his hurry to go.

Lazy Brownie is finally working!
He's trying to calm down the deer.
There's always so much excitement
At this special time of year.

The brownies are all finished loading
Christmas trees up on the sleigh.
How is Mrs. Santa helping
To speed them on their way?

George Hinke

There she is, in front of the castle.
"Just checking," I'm sure she would say.
That Teddy Bear needs two brownies
To lift him onto the sleigh.

Chief Brownie holds Santa's directions
That tell where the good children wait.
The reindeer are hitched to the sleigh —
They know they musn't be late.

Mrs. Santa is holding some earmuffs
And a scarf to keep Santa snug.
When Santa climbs into his sleigh,
He'll wrap up in that bright green rug.

Soon you'll hurry off to bed
On this marvelous magical night
When Santa sails through the sky
Leaving gifts before it gets light.

He'll fill your stockings with goodies
And pull a surprise from his pack.
Last of all, he'll nibble a cookie —
He's glad you left him a snack!

Now Santa must be off again
To yet another house —
Down the chimney
    and then back up —
As quiet as a mouse!

Now tired and happy, Santa's back home
The deer are brushed and fed.
Santa loves the kittens
In Lady Whiskers' bed.

The bells are rubbed and polished
(They're on ribbons made of silk).
Some brownies come downstairs to watch;
One pours the cat some milk.

COMET   CUPID   DONDER

Mrs. Santa has a tray
Of cocoa she's made ready.
One brownie shines up Santa's boots;
Another holds the reindeer steady.

Impy Brownie spilled some paint!
His pal is mopping up.
Santa settles back and says,
"I'd think I'd like a cup."

26
December

The brownies snuggle up in bed —
Or have a pillow fight!
Mrs. Claus brings cocoa;
She'll soon turn out the light.

Santa thinks of the good night's work
The brownies helped him do.
The brownies dream of heaps of toys
They've worked on all year through.

Now Santa's ready for some rest.
As he turns out the light,
He wishes every boy and girl

"Merry Christmas!"
and
"Good night!"